THIS BOOK IS FOR:

_____

FROM:

_____

"Dads are most
ordinary men
turned by love into
heroes, adventurers,
story-tellers, and
singers of song."

—PAM BROWN

BUSHEL
& PECK
BOOKS

Text copyright © 2021 by Mifflin Lowe
Illustrations copyright © 2021 by Dani Torrent

Published by Bushel & Peck Books
Fresno, California
www.bushelandpeckbooks.com

Bushel & Peck Books is dedicated to fighting illiteracy all over the world. For every
book we sell, we donate one to a child in need — book for book. To nominate a school or
organization to receive free books, please visit www.bushelandpeckbooks.com.

LCCN: 2020951234
ISBN: 9781733633567

First Edition

Printed in China

10 9 8 7 6 5 4 3 2 1

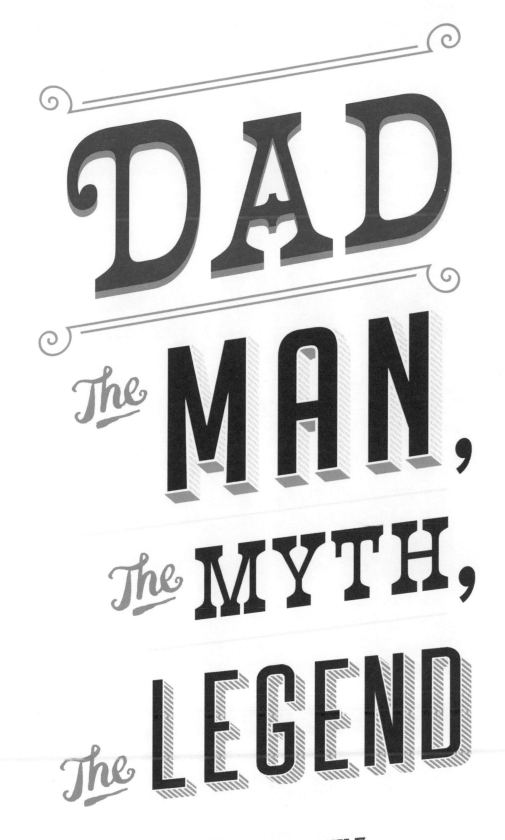

DAD

The MAN, The MYTH, The LEGEND

MIFFLIN LOWE

ILLUSTRATIONS BY
DANI TORRENT

Some say he's a myth. Others call him a legend. Mom says he's a legend in his **own** mind— whatever that means.

He's the one,
the only . . .

DAD!

Stronger than Sasquatch. More powerful than Thor! And when you're a kid like me, a dad like *that* can come in pretty handy.

Take last week. I was being squeezed by a **huge** python who hissed and spit in my face.

I gagged.

I gurgled.

I thought I was a **goner.**

"AAH EEH AH EEH

That's when Dad swung in and wrestled the beast to the ground!

In exactly three seconds . . .

... the python was completely *finito*!

Dad beat his chest.
"Me Tarzan!" he bellowed.

"Now Tarzan drive by hardware store," Mom said.

Drive? Uh-uh. See, Dad can fly!

"He just has to work on his landings," Mom says.
But even she admits those are pretty spectacular.

And that's not to say Dad **doesn't** drive. He says racing fuel runs in his veins!

But Mom says minivans **ARE NOT**
race cars. And for some reason, the
police always agree.

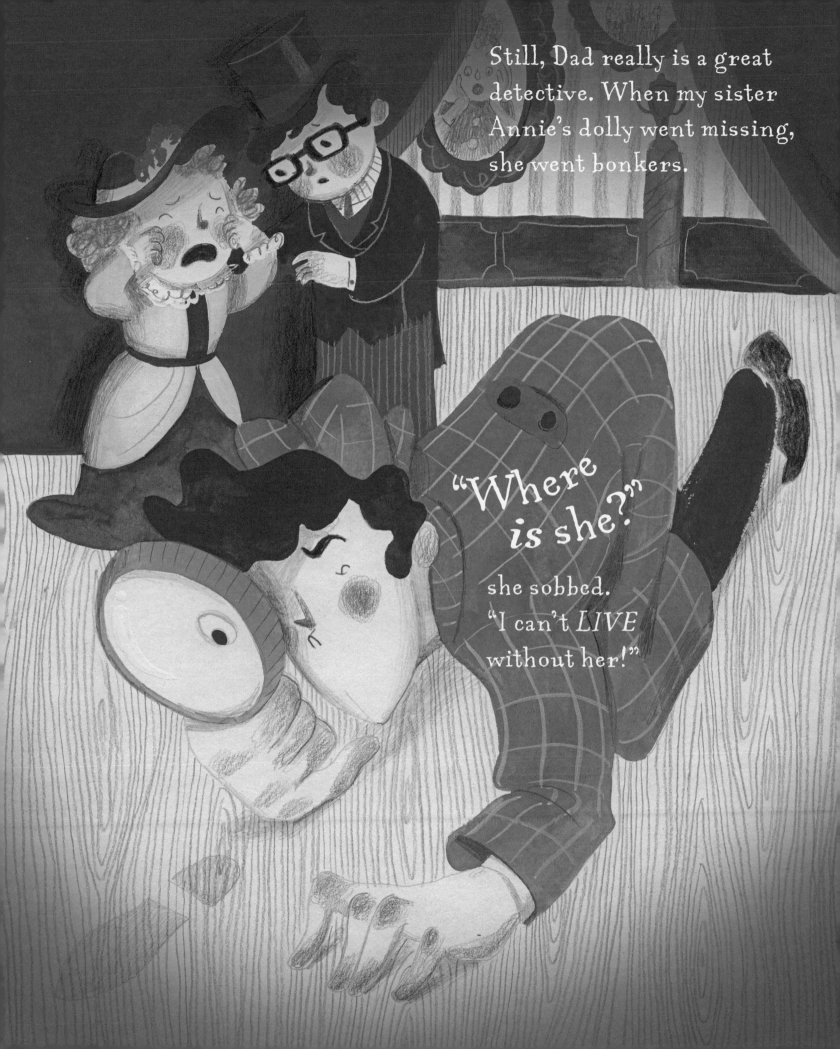

Still, Dad really is a great detective. When my sister Annie's dolly went missing, she went bonkers.

"Where is she?" she sobbed. "I can't *LIVE* without her!"

"**Elementary,**" Dad said. And just like that, there was Dolly! Amazing, right?

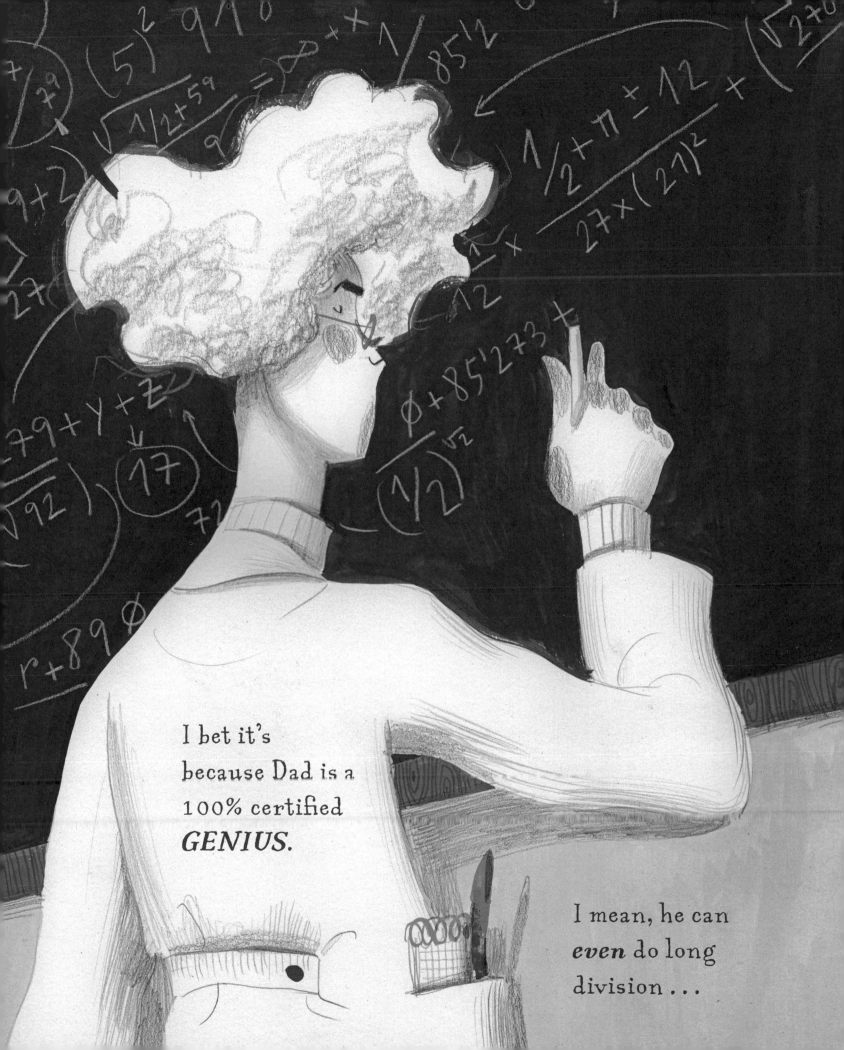

I bet it's because Dad is a 100% certified **GENIUS**.

I mean, he can **even** do long division . . .

... read books with
his eyes *closed* ...

. . . and once, he blasted us off into *space!* We went *so* high and *so* fast, he said we went where no kids have gone before.

Mom said if he pushes the swings that hard again, she'll send *him* where no one has gone before.

Sure, Dad
drives Mom
crazy sometimes,
but she says it
just makes her
crazy about *him*.

All I know is, I've seen enough kisses to
last me a *lifetime*. And I'm only ten!

Fortunately, Dad knows how to show he loves me in **other** ways. Like when I got the Terrible, Horrible Haircut and swore I wouldn't leave the house for a month?

Dad got one too.

"I'll bet everyone starts getting the Frankencut," he said.

And when my volcano set off the *sprinkler* system at the science fair, I thought they'd lock me up for a million years. But Dad just grinned.

"Now *that's* a volcano!!!"

he said.

And when my team lost
the game a zillion to one?

Dad knew just
how to make
things right.

It must be exhausting to be so amazing,
but somehow, he never gets tired.

Even when
I pin him.

Or beat him.

Or ask him to make my all-time
favorite dinner: spaghetti
with M&M's, chocolate sauce,
and . . . potato chips.

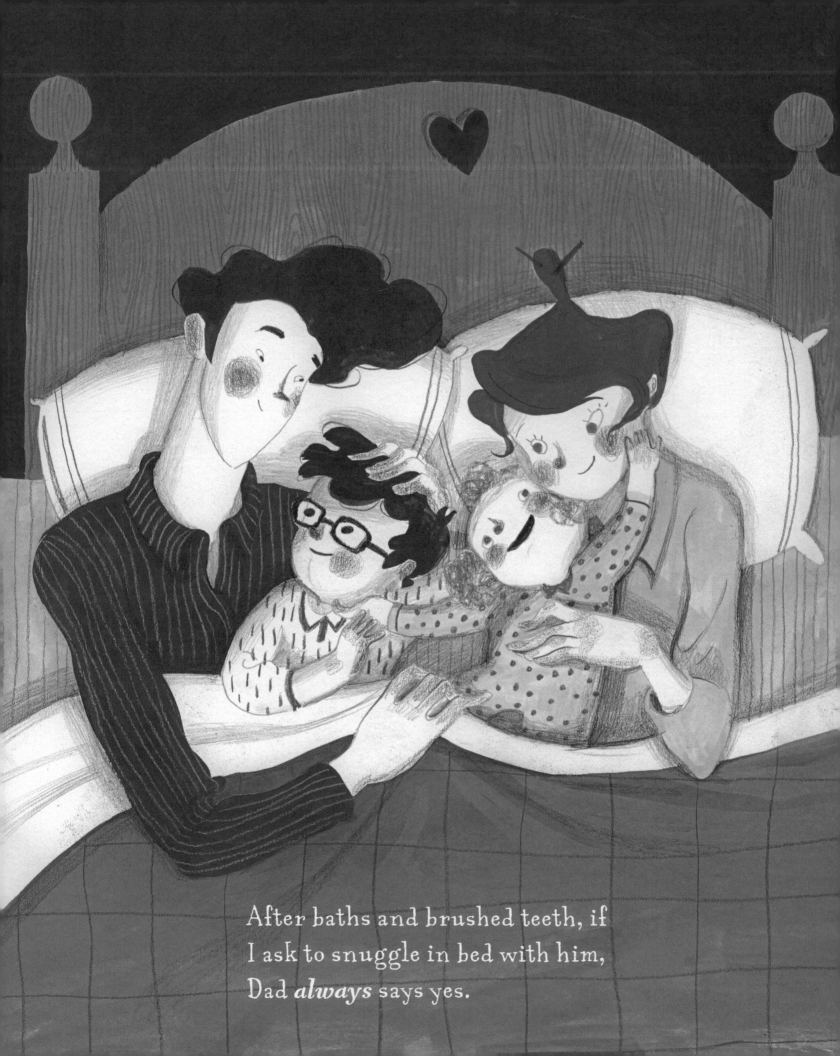

After baths and brushed teeth, if
I ask to snuggle in bed with him,
Dad *always* says yes.

It's then, just before I fall
asleep, that I hear him say my
favorite thing of all:

"Sleep tight, kiddo. And
remember to dream big,
because you can do *anything*."

With a dad like mine,
maybe I really can.

But you know what I'd
like to be most of all?

Just like him.

Now it's your turn. What are the things that make your dad so amazing to you? Write your own list here!